Based on the book written by Susan Ring
Adapted by Bill Scollon
Illustrated by Loter, Inc.

ABDOPUBLISHING.COM

Reinforced library bound edition published in 2019 by Spotlight, a division of ABDO, PO Box 398166, Minneapolis, Minnesota 55439. Spotlight produces high-quality reinforced library bound editions for schools and libraries. Published by agreement with Disney Press, an imprint of Disney Book Group.

Printed in the United States of America, North Mankato, Minnesota.
042018   092018

DISNEY PRESS
New York • Los Angeles

THIS BOOK CONTAINS
RECYCLED MATERIALS

Library of Congress Control Number: 2017960980

Publisher's Cataloging in Publication Data

Names: Scollon, Bill, author. | Ring, Susan, author. | Loter, Inc., illustrator.
Title: Mickey Mouse Clubhouse: Minnie's summer vacation / by Bill Scollon and Susan Ring; illustrated by Loter, Inc.
Description: Minneapolis, MN : Spotlight, 2019 | Series: World of reading level pre-1
Summary: Minnie and her friends all want to do different things on their vacation. She asks for Toodles to help find a way to make everyone happy.
Identifiers: ISBN 9781532141829 (lib. bdg.)
Subjects: LCSH: Mickey Mouse Clubhouse (Television program)--Juvenile fiction. | Mouse, Minnie (Fictitious character)--Juvenile fiction. | Vacations--Juvenile fiction. | Scheduling--Juvenile fiction. | Readers (Primary)--Juvenile fiction.
Classification: DDC [E]--dc23

Spotlight
A Division of ABDO
abdopublishing.com

Minnie is happy.
It is summer!

What do Minnie's friends want to do?

Mickey wants to swim.

Goofy wants to fish.

Daisy wants to swing.

Pluto wants to dig.

Donald wants to hike.

Minnie wants to take pictures.

Where can they do these things?

Minnie knows.
"We will go to Star Lake!"

Goofy can fish.

Mickey can swim.

Can Daisy swing?
Minnie calls Toodles.

Toodles can help.

Now Daisy can swing!

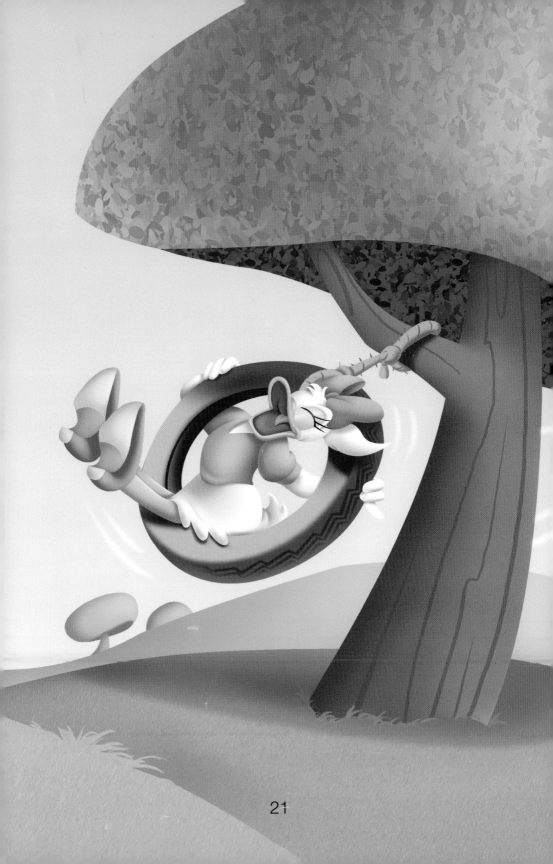

Can Pluto dig for a bone? No!

Minnie calls Toodles.

Toodles brings a map.
Now Pluto can dig!

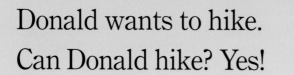

Donald wants to hike.
Can Donald hike? Yes!

Donald can hike up a hill!

Pluto digs.
He finds a bone.

Daisy swings.

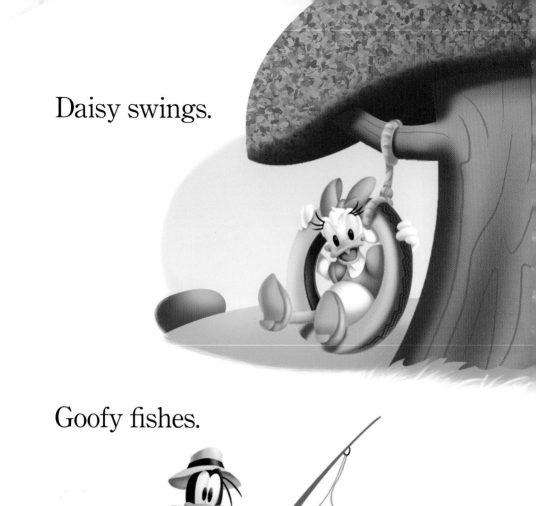

Goofy fishes.

Mickey swims.

Minnie takes pictures.
Happy summer!